Born in the beautiful Pacific Northwest and mother of two sons, Ann Loring is a retired kindergarten teacher who is very passionate about two things: children and the environment. After retirement, she combined her writing expertise with her paraeducator Boni Jo's drawing talent into a series of environmental children's picture books. She believes inspiring the interest and involvement of children in all aspects of environmental issues is the best way to ensure a better future for our planet.

Ann Loring

NESTER GNOME SAVES
THE PLANET BOOK 1

NO HUGS FOR LITTERBUGS

Sad Dilly

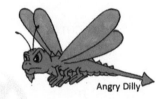

Angry Dilly

Happy Dilly

With Dilly
the Bearded
Dragon Fly

Illustrated By Boni Jo

AUSTIN MACAULEY PUBLISHERS™

LONDON · CAMBRIDGE · NEW YORK · SHARJAH

A CIP catalogue record for this title is available from the British Library.

ISBN 9781398431638 (Paperback)
ISBN 9781398431645 (Hardback)
ISBN 9781398431652 (ePub e-book)

www.austinmacauley.com

First Published (2021)
Austin Macauley Publishers Ltd
25 Canada Square
Canary Wharf
London
E14 5LQ

We would like to dedicate *Nester Gnome Saves the Planet: No Hugs for Litterbugs* to Pleasant Glade Elementary School in Olympia, WA, and to recognize both past and present staff and students as well as all the students worldwide that love and protect our environment.

We would like to thank Dr Melissa Luckow, retired botany professor, for sharing her extensive expertise on plant life and for providing information about the dependencies between insects and their individual habitats.

"Nester, can you please stop playing games," grumbled Hester, "and do something real?"

Nester paused his video game to look up. "I am. I'm really having fun!"

Hester glared even harder.

"Okay, tell me, what should I be doing, Hester?"

"Well, dear, look at this book. It may give you an idea."

"Help?" asked Nester. "What do you want me to help?"
"The entire Earth, Nester. I want you to read this book and then go save our planet!" Hester scowled. "Litterbugs need to be stopped!"

Whether a big dream that could change the world or a small dream that could fill the stomach, Nester the little forest gnome and his trusted friend, Dilly the bearded dragonfly, must remember...all dreams are possible if one just believes.

"Me? Do you see that, Hester? Your book says that the future of the planet depends on ME! I will make a difference."

"Nester, wait! Where are you going, and why are you taking Dilly with you? You know that bearded dragonfly of yours can't even talk."

Nester's answer was immediate. "My adventure will take me wherever I'm needed! I'm off to help the environment, one litterbug at a time. But Hester, I have one question. What is an environment?"

"Well, my dear, an environment is everything around us."

"Wow, everything...I understand now. I got this!"

As Nester opened the door, he turned to Hester and softly said, "Dilly will be my lookout, and Hester... I do believe."

"Hey bug! Can I ask you a question? By any chance are you a litterbug?"

While covering her ears, the bug grumbled, "Litterbug? Why would you think that? If anyone is a litterbug, I bet it's the guy who is making that horrible, terrible noise! I can't even enjoy my lunch!" Raising her voice even higher, she added, "Can't you see my lovely spotted wings? I am a ladybug. You may call me Lucy. I eat pesky aphids that kill these lovely roses. Without ladybugs, the world would not be so beautiful! And by the way, I hate noise! Please make it stop!"

"Let me go!" cried the bug. "My friends and I just escaped seventeen years of being trapped underground, and now we are celebrating our above-ground freedom as adults!" BZZZZZZZZZZZZZZZZZ!

"Stop! Please stop! You litterbugs are very irritating," Nester moaned. "Lucy and I don't appreciate all that noise."
"What? Who's Lucy?"
"Lucy is my ladybug friend, and my name is Nester. We are searching for litterbugs."
"Don't call us litterbugs. We are cicadas. My name is Calvin, and I am simply expressing my greatest joy. We are definitely not litterbugs. Keep looking."

"Wow! Listen to that! Hundreds of bugs, making almost as much noise as I do. I wonder what they are up to," said Calvin.

A few buzzed close to Nester, too close, causing him to start running and swatting at the swarming honey bees, while Dilly tried fiercely to protect Nester.

"Get away from us, you pesky litterbugs!" Nester cried. "You are scaring us!"

"Help!" Nester screamed, as an angry bee landed on his hand. "For heaven's sake! What's wrong with you? Have you got ants in your pants? You are causing an un-bee-lievable problem in our meadow!" yelled the bee.

"I...I...I just want to save our planet from litterbugs," mumbled Nester.

"I am bee-wildered! Us...litterbugs?" the bee buzzed. "Un-bee-lievable. Do I look anything like a litterbug? Do you even know anything about litterbugs?"

Nester sighed, "Well, not really, but I do know they are bad, very bad for the environment."

"My name is Bee-atrice, and I am the queen honey bee of our hive. Now, tell me, my dear fellow, do you like apples, squash, and bee-utiful blackberries?"
Nester smiled and cautiously nodded his head.
"Well," buzzed the queen bee, "then, you and the whole world need honey bees. Why? You may ask. Well, easy-beesy,"
winked Bee-atrice.

"See our tiny hairy legs and fuzzy bodies? Well, they're useful in gathering pollen. Flying from blossom to blossom, my worker bees stick their heads deep into all kinds of blossoms, drinking the sweet nectar, and getting pollen stuck all over themselves. That incredible combination not only feeds a whole bee colony, but when pollen is deposited on other blossoms, it becomes possible for all kinds of plants and trees to produce fruit, berries, and vegetables. It's called pollination. We feed the world."

"Yum! Thank you, honey bees. You definitely are good for the Earth and quite delicious too, but I know that litterbugs are out there; Hester's book says so, and we must keep searching so that the world remains bee-utiful!"

"Whoa! Finally! I found you!" Nester said while staring at the strangest-looking bug he had seen so far. "You are definitely a litterbug, aren't you?"

"I have no idea what you are talking about. Who or what are you anyway? I have never seen anything like you before," argued the large bug with two big bulgy eyes.

"My name is Nester. I am a forest gnome. Now it's your turn."

"Manny, my name is Manny, the praying mantis, and you are interfering with my hunting. Scram!"
"Not until you answer my question," demanded Nester. "Are you some weird kind of litterbug?"
"That's a big fat NO. You must be deaf. I told you I'm a praying mantis."
Backing away, Lucy timidly asked, "Just what do you eat?"
Scowling fiercely, Manny snapped, "Anything I want...Maybe you, little lady!"
In a flash, Lucy flew away.

"Bad, bad bug!" Nester scolded. "Why did you scare Lucy?"
"Lucy asked me a question, and I gave her an honest answer.
Anyway, she'd probably be very tough, but I'd be willing to give
her a try," said Manny, licking his lips.

"You think you can bully my friends, Manny?" Bee-atrice buzzed angrily. "Well, think again. I have something you don't have...and I will point it at you if you aren't careful."

"Wait, wait! I'm sorry," said Manny. "I'll do anything you want. Just no stingers, please."

"Can you promise to quit bullying and work on being a good friend?" Bee-atrice asked, stepping forward to shake Manny's hand.

"I can do that. Yes, I promise. No more bullying."

Manny stared at Nester, "And strange little man, I wish you luck in finding the litterbug."

Walking on into a large field of milkweed, Calvin smiled, "I know what those are, and they are not litterbugs!"
"Or praying mantises," laughed Bee-atrice.
Holding a tired Dilly, Nester exclaimed, "They are beautiful monarch butterflies! I am thrilled to see them, but I am also a little sad."

"How can those pretty monarchs make you sad?" asked Calvin.
"I feel sad because I honestly don't know what litterbugs look like,"
admitted Nester. "I may never find them. I may fail my quest to
help our environment."
Lucy grinned from antennae to antennae. "Tell me what you do
know about litterbugs."

"Hmmm, well," explained Nester, "I bet they are really mean and scary. They must have stingers or poison, and they are probably dangerous!"
"Oh dear! I'm not sure I want to help you find them. I'm scared!" Lucy shivered, before being distracted by the fluttering images above her head.

"Welcome to Milkweed Meadow. My name is Maas, and these are my two beautiful sisters, Melissa and Maynard. We recently hatched out of our chrysalises as butterflies, monarch butterflies to be exact."

"Chrysalis? That's a strange word," said Nester.

"Yes, it certainly is. A chrysalis is a hard case, kind of like a cradle holding and protecting a baby."

"Wow, that's amazing," began Nester. "Well, one thing is for sure... on our search for nasty litterbugs, we've made many interesting new friends...but none as pretty as you!"

"We certainly are glad you stumbled onto us because, you see, we monarchs need help." Maynard cried. "Lots of help!"Please understand that we are in danger of becoming extinct, and if things don't change soon, monarchs may no longer be around to dazzle you."

Maynard crunched up her tiny face and sobbed sadly. Maas fluttered his wing over her. Maynard cried even harder.

"That sounds bad." Nester looked at poor Maynard. "But I'm not quite sure what you are talking about. What does extinct mean?"

"All stages of the monarch's life depend on a single plant, milkweed. Milkweed has a milky juice and, of course, seed pods," explained Maas.

"I still don't understand about monarchs becoming, what was that word...?" Nester seemed embarrassed.

"Extinct," Maas frowned.

Tears running down her face, Maynard clarified. "It's simple. Our homes are our lives, and now people are destroying much of the monarch habitat. They spray poisonous chemicals, and they dig up the ground which wipes out not only common weeds but also our precious milkweed."

"Without milkweed, we'd have nothing to eat, nowhere to lay our eggs, and no nourishment to help us transform from caterpillars to butterflies. We'd die and become extinct," added Melissa.

"Die? We can't let that happen," mumbled Nester. "Show us how to plant more milkweed."Maas, Melissa, and Maynard nodded excitedly.

Soon the news of planting a new milkweed field traveled near and far.

Hester, along with many insect colonies, gathered at the empty field which was chosen to become the perfect location for a new milkweed meadow. Everyone was given a job, and everyone was anxious to get started.

"If we all protect the milkweed, we can help keep monarch butterflies in the world forever. Now, let's get started. Pick the pods; rake the dirt, and plant the milkweed seeds," instructed Nester.

Maynard smiled proudly while opening a pod.

Nester raked the soil. Melissa began spreading the seed.

Soon everyone was following their lead until the field was planted with milkweed. Friends helping friends make the world shine a little brighter, and teamwork can move a whole mountain instead of only a single rock.

Enjoying a job well done, the team found a picnic table to take a
much-deserved break. Hester watched as Dilly enjoyed the first
piece of her delicious apple pie. Nester began unwrapping his
chocolate bar, but then the unthinkable happened. Looking on in
disbelief, Hester watched as a candy wrapper flew carelessly out
of her husband's hand to the ground. She opened her mouth to
speak, but all that came out was, "N-o-o-o!"

"Well, Nester, you did it!
You finally found a
litterbug, and

"No, not me!" moaned Nester. "I can't be a litterbug. I love the environment, the world, and the whole entire planet.
I need to fix this!"
"My dear Nester, you are a good person," reassured Hester. "But you can also be very careless, and yes, today you are a litterbug." Staring at Nester's horrified face, Hester added, "So, what do you say? We can all work in teams to clean up the litter in both the meadow and in our beautiful forest."
"Yes!" cheered Nester. "I'll do anything to make it up to the environment."

"Working together with your friends, you can make the world a cleaner and healthier place for all to live! Help us put an end to littering!"

"Now I know what a litterbug is! It is any living person or creature that carelessly throws trash onto the ground or into the water." Nester nodded to Hester and Dilly and said, "Believe me, that person will never again be me!

For additional information, Google the following topics:
- Litter Free Activity Book
- Littering guide for kids
- How does littering affect the environment
- Littering coloring pictures

CPSIA information can be obtained
at www.ICGtesting.com
Printed in the USA
LVHW071312030621
689240LV00006B/101

9 781398 431638